Puss in Boots

My First Reading Book

Story retold by Janet Brown
Illustrations by Ken Morton

ARMADILLO

The miller's three sons live in an old mill house. The oldest son owns the mill. The middle son owns the donkey. And the youngest son owns nothing but his father's cat.

"Alas!" says the youngest son. "I am too poor to feed you, little Puss."

"Never fear," says Puss. "Buy me a pair of boots and a bag, and I will make our fortune."

The youngest son is so surprised, he spends his last pennies on the cat.

What does the cat ask the miller's third son to buy for him?

Puss pulls on his boots and catches a large rabbit!
Then he slings the bag over his shoulder and goes
to the palace.

"I am Puss in Boots!" he tells the King. "I bear you a
present from my Lord, the Marquis of Carrabas!"

"A talking cat?" says the King. "Now fancy that! Tell
your Lord I accept his gift, with thanks."

Who does Puss tell the King that his master is?

Next, Puss in Boots catches two fat partridges! Then he slings the bag over his shoulder and goes to the palace.

"I am Puss in Boots!" he tells the King. "I bear you a present from my Lord, the Marquis of Carrabas!"

"What a generous fellow this Marquis is, "says the King. "Tell him I accept his gift, with thanks."

What is the second present that Puss takes for the King?

Then Puss in Boots leads the miller's son to the river.

"You must go for a swim," "he says. "And when the King and his beautiful daughter pass by, you must agree with everything I say."

When the King's carriage passes, Puss runs into the road. "Help!" he cries. "Robbers have stolen my Lord's clothes!"

"Dear me," says the King. "We can't have a naked Marquis in the streets! Servants, fetch my finest suit for this young man!"

Soon the miller's son is dressed in royal clothes and riding in the royal carriage with the King and his beautiful daughter.

Why does the King send his servants to fetch his finest suit?

Puss in Boots runs ahead. He sees some mowers in a lush, green meadow.

"The King is coming!" he tells them. "You must tell him that this meadow belongs to the Marquis of Carrabas." And he gives them some money.

He sees some reapers in a ripe, golden cornfield.

"The King is coming!" he tells them. "You must tell him that this cornfield belongs to the Marquis of Carrabas." And he gives them some money.

What does Puss ask the mowers to do?

When the King's carriage passes by, the King asks, "Who owns this fine meadow?"

"Our Lord, the Marquis of Carrabas," reply the mowers, bowing deeply.

When the carriage moves on, the King asks, "Who owns this fine cornfield?"

"Our Lord, the Marquis of Carrabas," reply the reapers, bowing deeply.

By now the King is very impressed indeed.

Why do you think the King is very impressed?

Meanwhile Puss in Boots has reached the great castle of a nasty ogre.

"I've heard how clever you are," Puss tells the ogre. "Can you *really* turn yourself into an animal?"

The ogre turns himself into a wild, ferocious lion. "Of course," he roars.

Puss leaps on top of a cupboard. "Do you do small animals as well?" he asks politely.

The ogre turns himself into a teeny, tiny mouse. "Of course," he squeaks proudly.

Puss leaps on the mouse and gobbles him up!

What animals does the ogre turn himself into?

When the King's carriage arrives at the ogre's castle, Puss in Boots cries, "Welcome to the home of my Lord, the Marquis of Carrabas"

The King turns to the miller's son.

"What a splendid fellow you are," he says. "You have a clever cat, you bring me presents, you own all the best land, and you live in the finest castle in my kingdom. You are the perfect husband for my daughter!"

Why does the King want the miller's son to marry his daughter?

So the miller's son becomes a prince, marries a princess, and lives happily ever after in the ogre's castle.

And the clever Puss? He hangs up his boots, and lies purring by the fire to this very day.

Now that his work is done, what does Puss like to do all day?

Look carefully at the two pictures below. There are ten differences between them. Can you spot them?

1. Top of throne   2. Leg of throne   3. King's beard   4. King's crown   5. Detail on King's cape   6. Detail on King's trousers   7. Window frame   8. Brick on wall   9. Stripe on Puss's tail   10. Buckle on Puss's boot